The Titanic and Other Shipping Disasters

George Ivanoff

Contents

Danger on the Water

Humans have been travelling across water for as long as there has been recorded history. Like any form of travel, venturing out onto an ocean, lake or river comes with risk. Accidents happen and disaster can strike – from a **capsizing** rowboat to a sinking passenger **liner**.

This ancient Roman artwork shows a person rowing on the Nile river in Egypt.

A common factor among many shipping disasters is human error. People make mistakes – they make poor decisions, they get distracted, or they forget to do something important. Mistakes like this can lead to problems. And problems out on the water can lead to disaster.

The wreck of the *Atun* fishing boat lies in the ocean off the coast of Papua New Guinea.

The *Cataraqui*, August 1845

Striking a Reef

Built in Quebec, Canada, in 1840, the *Cataraqui* (pronounced *cat-ar-ah-kwee*) was a 73-metre-long "barque", which is a type of sailing ship. The wrecking of the *Cataraqui* in 1845 is Australia's deadliest **civil** shipping disaster.

The *Cataraqui* set sail from Liverpool in England on 20 April 1845 to bring **emigrants** to Melbourne. It had a crew of 44 and was carrying 367 passengers. During its long voyage, seven people died and five babies were born, so when disaster struck, there were 409 people on board.

The Wreck of the *Cataraqui*

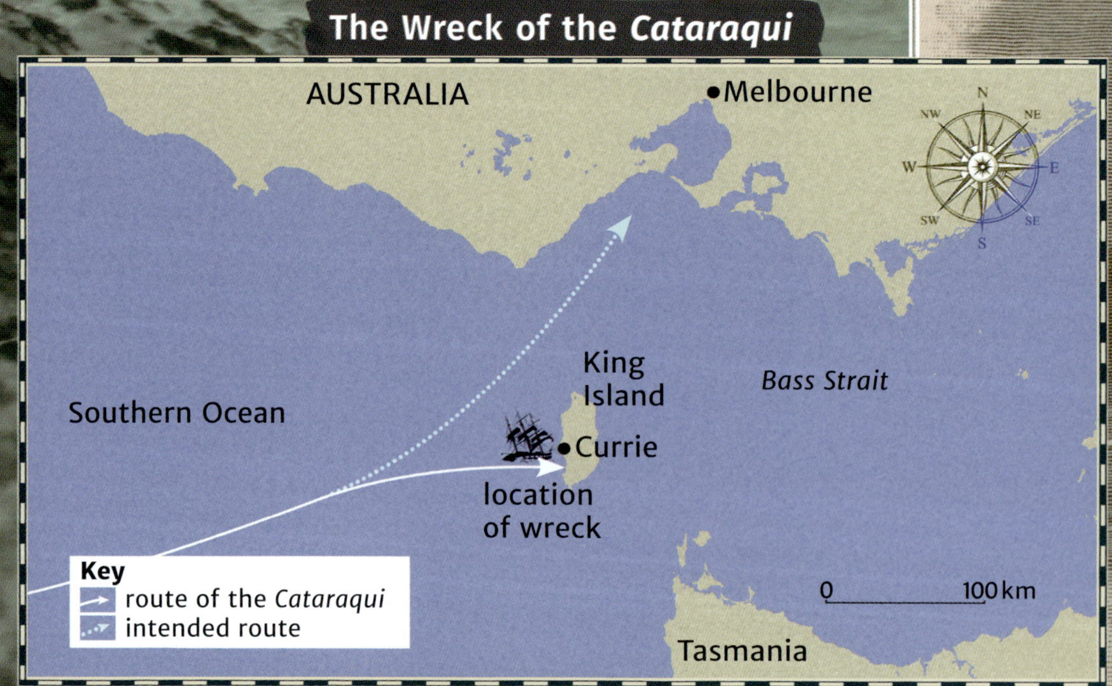

After two weeks of heavy weather in the Southern Ocean, the *Cataraqui* sailed into Bass Strait during a bad storm. The ship struck a reef on the west coast of King Island at 4:30 am on 4 August 1845. It took many hours for the ship to break apart and sink, but the bad weather made escape to shore extremely difficult. Even though the ship was only 100 metres from shore (near what is now the town of Currie), 400 people died. Only one of the passengers and eight of the crew survived.

This illustration shows the wreck of the *Cataraqui* off King Island.

Human Error

Sailors used sextants to calculate where they were on a map.

Navigating at sea in the nineteenth century was difficult, as it involved observing the Sun, Moon, planets and stars, then taking measurements with a special instrument called a **sextant**. The storms that the *Cataraqui* was sailing through made navigation even more difficult. When entering Bass Strait, the ship's **navigator** miscalculated the position of the ship. The *Cataraqui* was 160 kilometres off course, meaning it was a long way from the route the navigator had planned. This meant the ship's captain had no idea they were so close to the reef.

This monument on King Island marks the burial place of 206 passengers of the *Cataraqui*.

What If?

What if the navigator on board the *Cataraqui* had double-checked his calculations? Imagine how differently things might have turned out if the crew had known they were off course.

A broken piece of the *Cataraqui* wreck lies on the bottom of the ocean.

The *Princess Alice*, September 1878

Drowning in Sewage

Built in Greenock, Scotland, in 1865, the *Princess Alice* was a **paddle steamer**. It carried passengers along the Thames (pronounced *tems*) River in England in the 1860s and 1870s.

On 3 September 1878, the *Princess Alice* was travelling along the Thames River, returning to London from the seaside town of Sheerness. It was carrying over 700 people, including passengers and crew.

The Wreck of the *Princess Alice*

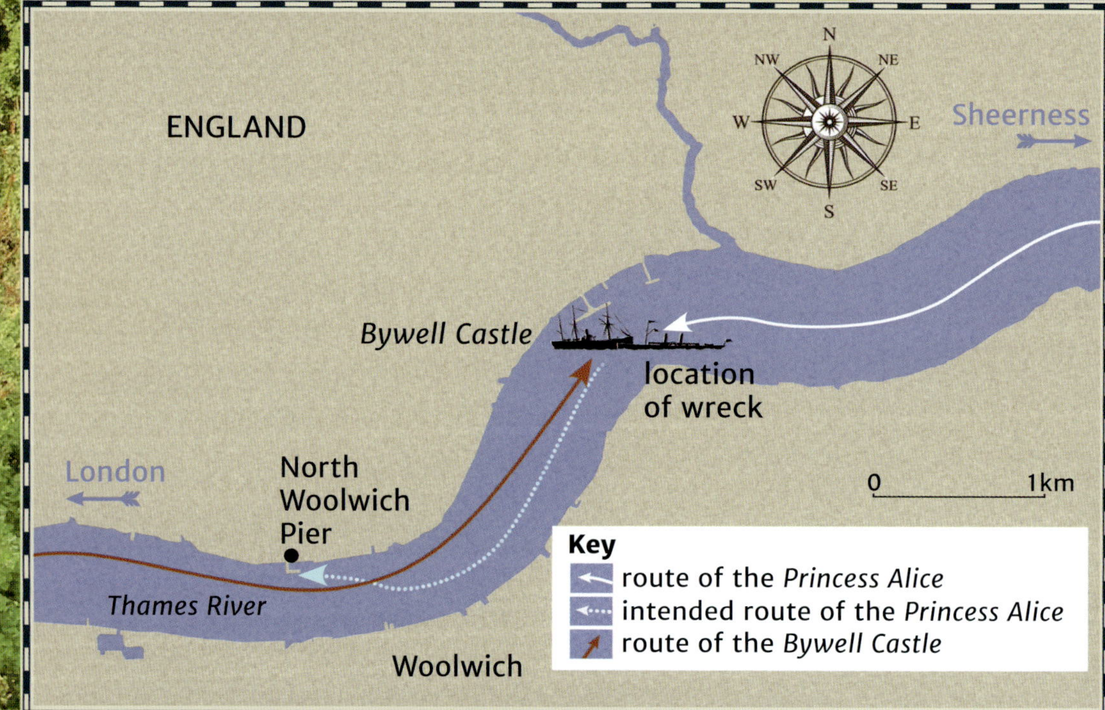

At about 7:45 pm, it collided with a cargo ship carrying coal, the *Bywell Castle*, travelling in the opposite direction. The larger ship hit the *Princess Alice* on its starboard side (right-hand side), slicing it in two and causing it to sink.

The collision happened near a series of **sewage** outlets, and the crew and passengers were plunged into a waste-filled river in the dark. The crew on board the *Bywell Castle* put boats, **lifebuoys** and ropes into the water to try to rescue them. Although some people were rescued, approximately 640 people died. Exact numbers are not known, because there was no passenger list for the *Princess Alice*.

This illustration of the *Princess Alice* collision appeared in a London newspaper after the accident.

Human Error

The cause of this shipping disaster was entirely human error. The crew of the *Princess Alice* did not follow waterway rules. When spotting an oncoming ship, they should have turned to the right of it – which is what the crew of the *Bywell Castle* would have expected them to do. Instead, they turned left, bringing the *Princess Alice* directly into the path of the other ship. The crew of the *Bywell Castle* also contributed to the accident by not stopping their engines quickly enough.

This disaster led to emergency signalling lights being installed on all British boats.

the *Bywell Castle*

the *Princess Alice*

What If?

What if the crew of the *Princess Alice* had followed waterway rules and turned right instead of left? Imagine all those lives saved by one decision.

A monument stands in the town of Woolwich, England, dedicated to those who died aboard the *Princess Alice*.

The *Doña Paz*, December 1987

Fire on Water

The *Doña Paz* (pronounced *don-ya paz*) was a passenger ferry originally named the *Himeyuri Maru* (pronounced *hi-meh-yuri ma-roo*) when it was built in Hiroshima, Japan, in 1963. It was later used for ferrying passengers in the Philippines and was renamed the *Doña Paz*.

On 20 December 1987, the *Doña Paz* left Leyte Island, heading for the Philippines capital of Manila. It was carrying over 4000 passengers.

The Wreck of the *Doña Paz*

At 10:30 pm that night, while travelling along the Tablas Strait, the ferry collided with the **oil tanker** MT *Vector*. The collision started a fire, and the ferry went up in flames before finally sinking two hours later. Most of the passengers and crew from both ships died in the fire or from drowning – over 4000 people from the *Doña Paz* and 11 from the MT *Vector*. Only 25 passengers from the *Doña Paz* and 2 crew members from the MT *Vector* were rescued.

The sinking of the *Doña Paz* is the deadliest civil shipping disaster of all time.

This is an artist's imagining of the collision between the *Doña Paz* and the MT *Vector*.

Human Error

The collision between the ferry and the oil tanker was caused by human error, and an investigation decided it was the fault of the crew of the MT *Vector*. They were not following safety procedures and may not have had a crew member stationed as **lookout** at the time of the accident. The oil tanker was also found to be "unseaworthy" (not in good enough condition to be at sea) and did not have a licence.

However, the crew of the *Doña Paz* also contributed to the disaster. There were no senior crew members on duty at the time of the collision. The ship was under the control of a junior crew member, who did not see the MT *Vector* in time.

The *Doña Paz* waited in port at Tacloban before setting sail to Manila.

Human error also contributed to the number of deaths. The *Doña Paz* was severely overcrowded, carrying more than twice the number of people it was supposed to. There wasn't a record of all the passengers, which is why the death toll for this disaster is only estimated. With none of the senior *Doña Paz* crew on duty, there was no one to give passengers instructions on what to do after the collision.

What If?

What if the *Doña Paz* had not been overcrowded? What if the the MT *Vector* had stationed a crew member as lookout? Would the collision still have happened?

This wreath was laid on the water in the Tablas Strait in 2017 to remember the victims of the *Doña Paz* wreck.

The *Exxon Valdez*, March 1989

Oil Spill

The *Exxon Valdez* was a huge oil tanker ship known as a "supertanker". Built in 1986, it was owned and operated by the American oil and gas company Exxon.

On the evening of 23 March 1989, the *Exxon Valdez* left the city of Valdez in Alaska, USA, to deliver oil to California. At 12:04 am that night, the tanker ran aground on the Bligh Reef in Prince William Sound, an inlet in the Gulf of Alaska. Running aground meant that, although the ship wasn't wrecked, it was stuck on the rocks that made up the reef.

The Wreck of the *Exxon Valdez*

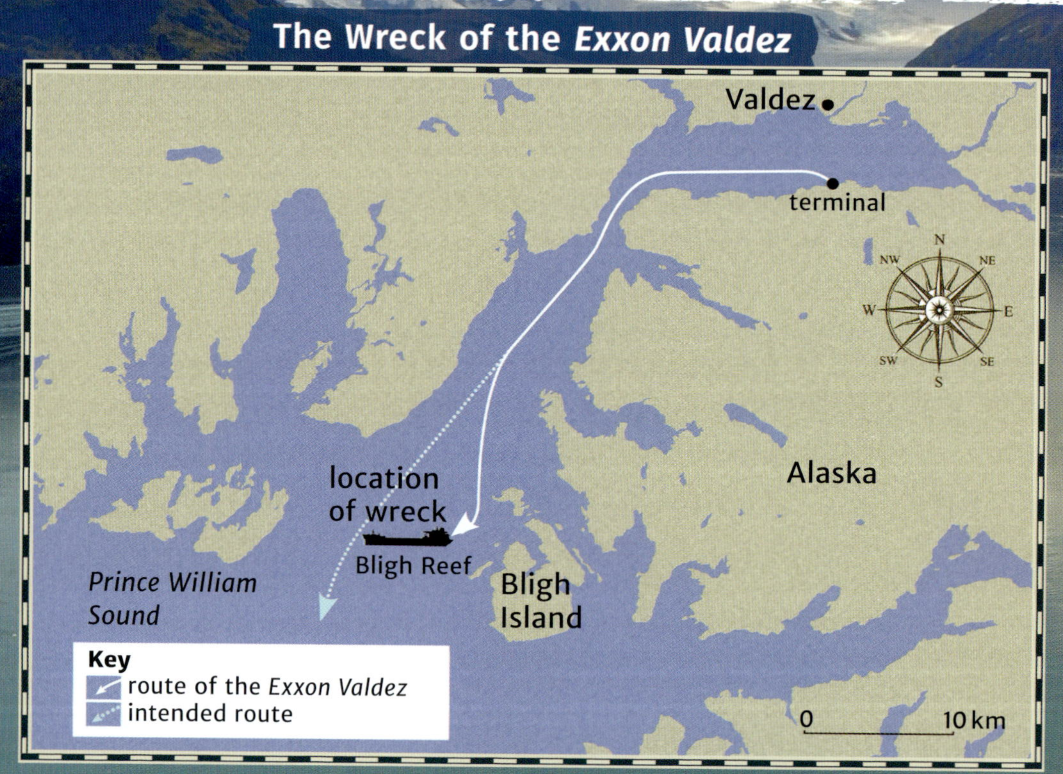

Eight out of the 11 cargo holds were punctured by the rocks, spilling almost 42 million litres of oil. The ship eventually had to be towed away by two tugboats.

Although none of the crew were injured, the accident was a huge environmental disaster. The coastline had been a pristine, unpolluted area home to many species of wildlife. The spill polluted over 2000 kilometres of shoreline and the waters around it. Large numbers of native wildlife were killed. Many were poisoned by the oil. Birds covered in oil were unable to fly, and died.

Wildlife Toll

- 250 000 seabirds
- 2800 sea otters
- 300 harbor seals
- 250 bald eagles
- 22 orcas
- an unknown number of salmon and herring

This oil-covered bird was rescued on an island in Prince William Sound.

There were also ongoing effects on the environment because **microorganisms**, such as plankton, were destroyed. This left many surviving animals with a reduced supply of food.

There was a large clean-up campaign. Helicopters were used to spray the area with special chemicals that helped to dissolve and disperse the oil. There was also a rescue operation to save animals that were covered in the oil and still alive.

The *Exxon Valdez* was repaired, renamed the *Exxon Mediterranean*, and continued to be used as an oil tanker.

Some of the oil was removed using special equipment called "booms" (floating physical barriers to contain oil) and "skimmers" (used to skim oil off the water's surface).

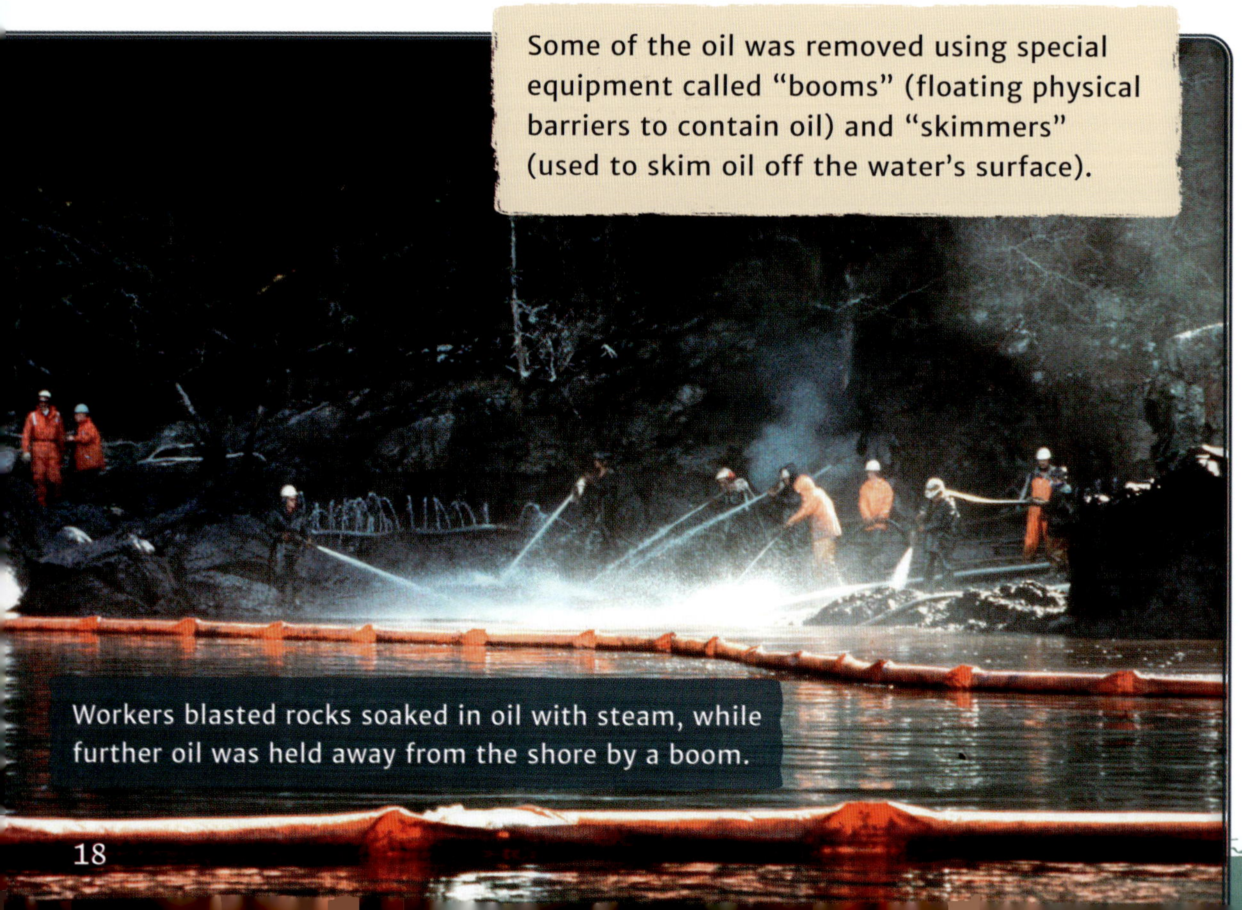

Workers blasted rocks soaked in oil with steam, while further oil was held away from the shore by a boom.

Human Error

The disaster was a result of human error on the part of the *Exxon Valdez* crew, and of the Exxon Corporation management.

The crew were understaffed and overworked. The captain was asleep at the time of the accident, leaving the **third mate** in charge. He was the only officer on duty for most of the night, which was against the rules. He was tired and he incorrectly steered the ship as it approached the reef. He had also been unable to use the special collision-avoidance radar on the ship, because it was broken and had not been repaired by the company before the voyage.

What If?

What if the captain of the *Exxon Valdez* had been in charge that night? What if the collision-avoidance radar had been repaired when it should have been? Imagine how these decisions might have prevented a massive environmental disaster.

The oil from the *Exxon Valdez* spread across the surface of the water of Prince William Sound.

The *Costa Concordia*, January 2012

Striking Rocks

Launched in 2005, the *Costa Concordia* was an Italian cruise ship, meaning a ship designed for leisure trips. It was 290 metres long with 13 passenger decks. It had luxury facilities including restaurants, four swimming pools and a poolside movie theatre.

On 13 January 2012, the *Costa Concordia* set off on a seven-day cruise through the Tyrrhenian (pronounced *ty-ren-ee-an*) Sea, along the coast of Italy. It carried 3206 passengers and 1023 crew.

The Wreck of the *Costa Concordia*

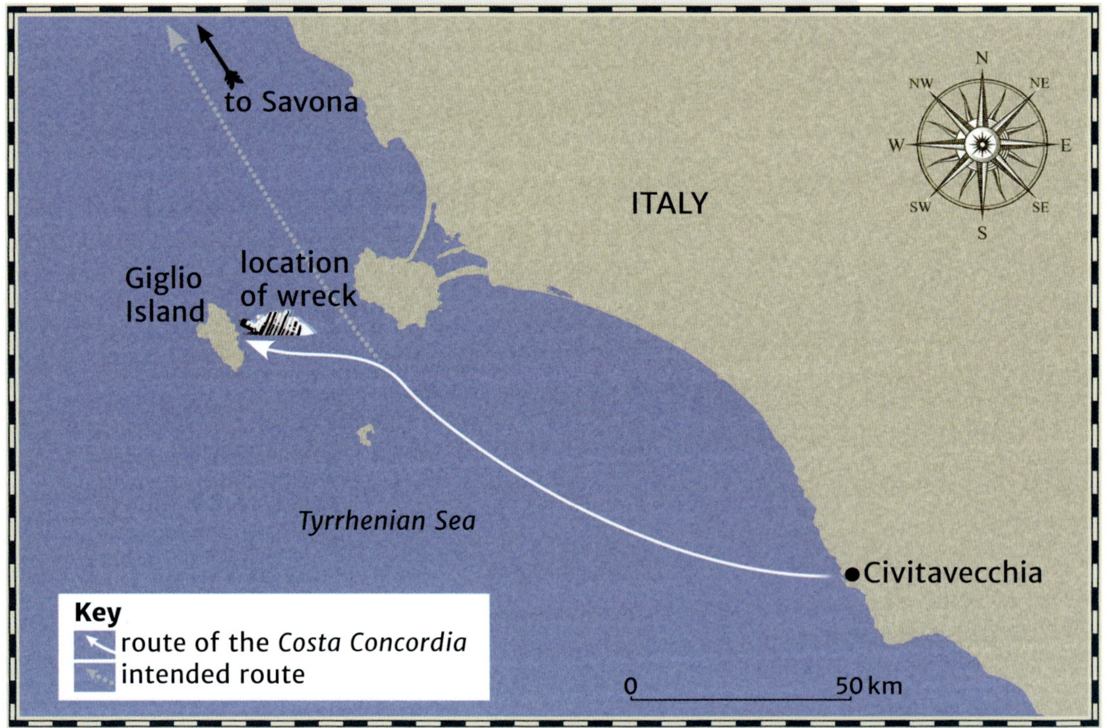

Roughly two hours into the cruise, the captain changed course to pass closer to Giglio Island, greeting a former captain there by sounding the ship's horn.

At about 9:45 pm, the cruise ship struck rocks. The port side (left side) of the ship's **hull** was torn open and it began to fill with water. The crew were not able to steer the ship, and as the *Costa Concordia* took on water, wind overturned it onto its side. Lifeboats were launched, and the captain called for the ship to be evacuated just before 11 pm.

A huge rescue operation was mounted. Most of the people onboard were rescued, but 32 people died.

The capsized *Costa Concordia* lay half-sunken off the coast of Giglio Island for years.

Human Error

An investigation after the disaster found the captain of the *Costa Concordia* to be at fault. It was his decision to change course, bringing the ship too close to the island. The situation was made more dangerous as it was night-time, and the cruise ship was travelling at high speed.

When put on **trial**, the captain tried to blame the helmsman (the person who steers the ship). He said the helmsman did not follow his orders after the rocks were spotted, causing the ship to crash. But when a court found that the helmsman could not have prevented the collision, the captain was found guilty of causing the accident and sentenced to 16 years in prison.

The captain of the *Costa Concordia* was found guilty of causing the deaths of 32 passengers.

What If?

What if the captain had kept the *Costa Concordia* on course? Imagine how this one decision could have prevented disaster.

The *Costa Concordia* was finally turned upright again in 2013, revealing the massive damage to its side from the collision.

The *Titanic*, April 1912

Iceberg Collision

On 10 April 1912, the passenger ship *Titanic* set out on her **maiden voyage** from England to America. There were over 2200 passengers and crew on board.

At 11:35 pm on 14 April 1912, while travelling through the Atlantic Ocean, Frederick Fleet, a crewman who was on duty as lookout, spotted an iceberg ahead. **First Officer** William Murdoch ordered the ship to turn left and put its engines in reverse to avoid a collision, but it was too late. At 11:40 pm, the starboard side of the *Titanic* scraped along the iceberg, damaging the hull. Five of the *Titanic*'s supposedly watertight **compartments** ruptured and began to take on water.

The Wreck of the *Titanic*

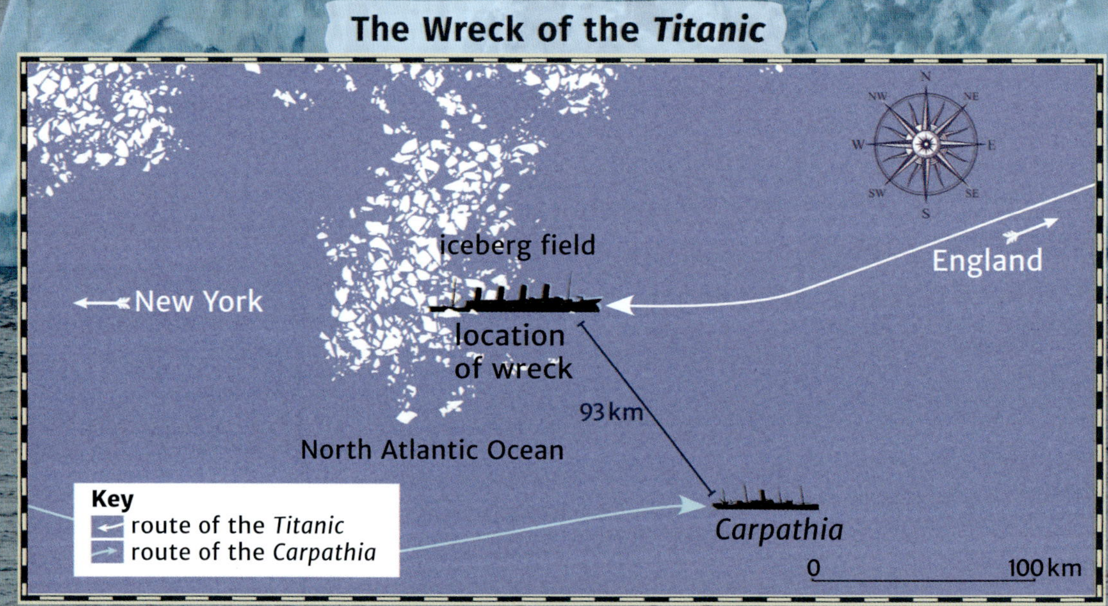

A **distress signal** was sent, but the first lifeboats were not launched until 12:45 am on 15 April, taking only women and children. Many of the lifeboats were carrying far fewer people than they could have. Most passengers didn't realise they were in danger until it was too late. After all the lifeboats were gone, many people jumped into the freezing water.

It took the *Titanic* several hours to sink. As the compartments filled with water, the **bow** of the ship sank into the water, pulling the **stern** up out of the water. The strain on the ship caused it to break in half. The bow half of the ship sank first, with the stern following. The ship finally sank completely at 2:20 am.

It was not until 3:30 am that the passenger ship *Carpathia* arrived in answer to the distress signal. Only 705 people survived the sinking.

The sinking of the *Titanic* was shown in this 1912 painting by artist Willy Stöwer.

Human Error

There was much human error involved with the disaster of the *Titanic.* The ship was considered unsinkable, so the owners decided it would only carry 20 lifeboats instead of the 48 needed to accommodate all the passengers. The owners thought that 20 lifeboats would be enough to go back and forth, carrying passengers to a rescue ship if the *Titanic* was ever damaged.

Long before the *Titanic* struck the iceberg, the ship received warnings of icebergs in the area from other ships. Although the captain, Edward Smith, changed the course of the ship a little, he made the decision not to slow down. Running at full speed was standard practice and the captain saw no reason to change this. More warning messages that came in the evening were not even passed on to the captain.

Captain Edward Smith

First Officer William Murdoch

Frederick Fleet, lookout

When the iceberg was spotted by lookout Frederick Fleet, First Officer William Murdoch turned the ship, which resulted in it scraping across the iceberg with its starboard side. The ship would have had a better chance of survival if it had hit the iceberg head-on.

What If?

What if the additional warnings had been delivered and the *Titanic's* captain had slowed the ship? What if the first officer hadn't turned the ship as it approached the iceberg? Imagine how different things would have been if the *Titanic* had hit the iceberg, but not sunk.

This iceberg, photographed the same day the *Titanic* sank, was thought to be the one the ship hit.

The Titanic
The Ship of Dreams

The *Titanic* was built for a shipping company called the White Star Line, in Belfast, Ireland. Construction took three years and was completed in April 1912.

The *Titanic* was the largest and most luxurious ship of its time, measuring about 269 metres in length with 10 decks. It had three engines powered by steam and coal.

Passengers aboard the ship were divided into three areas. The first-class area on the upper decks had private suites, each with two bedrooms and a bathroom. There was a fancy dining room with a live orchestra which played during meals, as well as lots of other facilities, including a swimming pool, a squash court and a barber shop.

First-class passengers enjoyed dinner in the *Titanic's* dining room.

The *Titanic* departed Southampton, England, on 10 April 1912.

The second-class area on the lower decks had rooms with two or four beds each, mostly bunk beds. The facilities weren't as fancy as first class, but they still had things like an outdoor walking area, a dining room with a pianist at mealtimes, a barber shop and a library.

The third-class area (called steerage) was on the lowest passenger decks near the engines. It had much more basic facilities. Rooms had up to ten beds. There was a small dining room with simple food and a general room with a piano.

the *Titanic*'s grand staircase

The *Titanic* was nicknamed "The Ship of Dreams" and the White Star Line claimed that it was the safest ship of all time. It could carry over 2000 passengers and needed a crew of about 900. Sadly, because everyone thought that the ship was unsinkable, it only carried 20 lifeboats capable of saving just over 1000 people.

Neither its size nor its luxurious interior would prove to be any help to the *Titanic* and its passengers when it struck ice on its fateful first voyage.

The White Star Line advertised their ships the *Titanic* and the *Olympic* as "the largest steamers in the world".

There are many things that can contribute to a shipping disaster – weather conditions, rough water, war or simply bad luck. In most cases, there is also an element of human error. Sometimes, people make mistakes, resulting in a situation becoming worse than it otherwise would have been. An iceberg was the cause of the *Titanic* disaster, but the captain's decision to not slow down and the first officer's choice to turn the ship also contributed.

Sometimes, as with the *Princess Alice* and *Costa Concordia* disasters, the fault is entirely with the people. In these cases, the ships would have been completely safe if not for the poor decisions that were made.

Imagine how many shipping disasters might have been prevented or lessened if human error was not involved.

The sunken bow of the *Titanic* is a reminder of history's worst shipping disasters.

Glossary

bow (*noun*) the front of a ship or boat

capsizing (*verb*) turning upside down in water

civil (*adjective*) not military

compartments (*noun*) areas of a ship that can be sealed off to stop the ship from filling with water

distress signal (*noun*) a message sent by a ship to request help

emigrants (*noun*) people who leave their own country to permanently move to another country

first officer (*noun*) the second most senior person on a ship after the captain; also called first mate

hull (*noun*) the main part or body of a ship

lifebuoys (*noun*) inflated supports that help people float

liner (*noun*) a large passenger ship designed for comfort

lookout (*noun*) a person who watches for danger ahead

maiden voyage (*noun*) the first official journey of a ship

microorganisms (*noun*) tiny living things

navigator (*noun*) a person who plans the course of a ship

oil tanker (*noun*) a ship designed to carry large amounts of oil

paddle steamer (*noun*) a river boat with large paddle wheels, propelled by steam

sewage (*noun*) waste water

sextant (*noun*) a tool for measuring angles, used in navigation

stern (*noun*) the back of a ship or boat

third mate (*noun*) the fourth most senior person on a ship, after the captain, first mate and second mate

trial (*noun*) when a case is heard in court to decide if a person has broken a law

Index